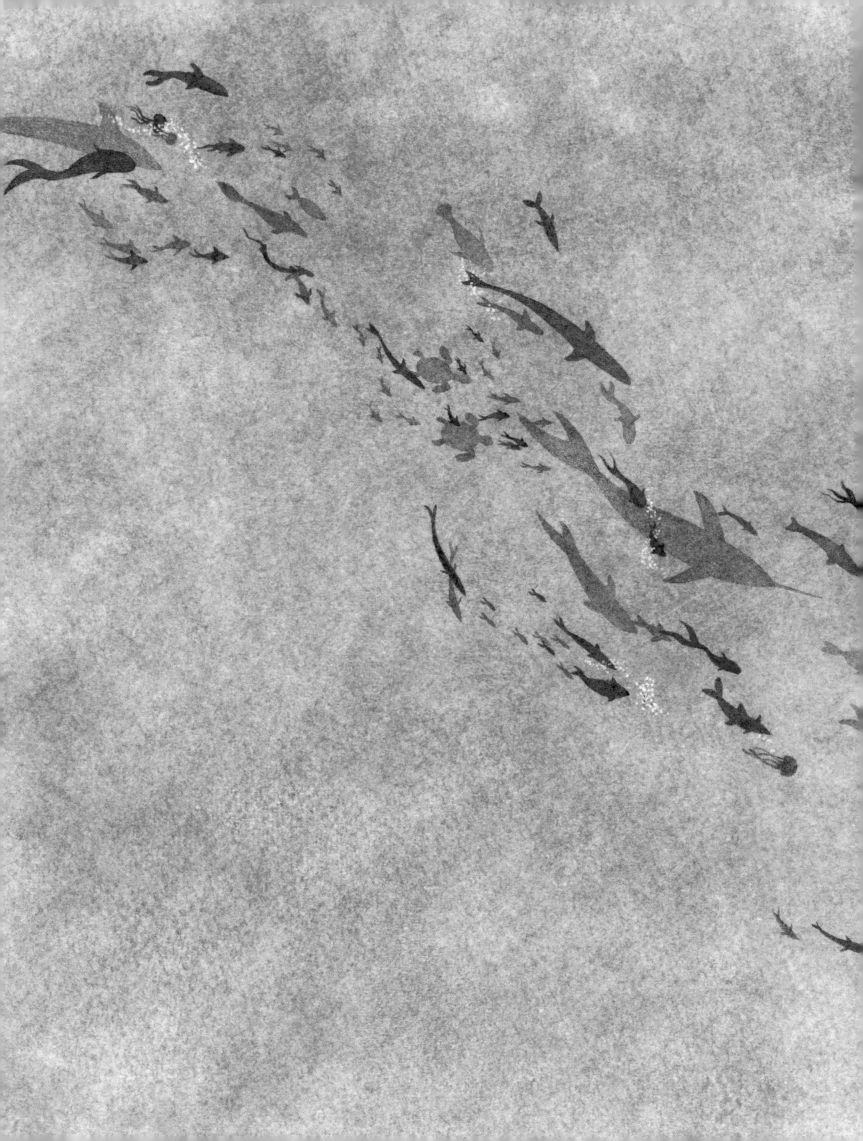

THE
SEA
TIGER

For Neil

A TEMPLAR BOOK

First published in hardback and softback in the UK in 2014 by Templar Publishing,
an imprint of The Templar Company Limited,
Deepdene Lodge, Deepdene Avenue, Dorking, Surrey, RH5 4AT, UK
www.templarco.co.uk

ISBN 978-1-78370-006-6 (hardback)
ISBN 978-1-78370-007-3 (softback)

Edited by Katie Cotton

Printed in China

THE
SEA
TIGER

VICTORIA TURNBULL

templar publishing

I am the Sea Tiger.

And this is Oscar.

I am Oscar's best friend. We do everything together.

Where I lead, Oscar follows.

Every day is a different

adventure under

the sea.

We ride the ocean current over shells and
sea horses and strange-coloured fish.
It takes us to the most extraordinary places.

In the circus shell,

we fly…

… and on the carousel,

we spin until we're dizzy.

When we're together,

anything is possible.

After a day full of adventure and a bellyful of fish, we're ready for bed.

Sometimes

we

fall

straight

to

sleep.

Sometimes I have to

scare the monsters away.

And sometimes,
for no particular
reason, we hitch
a ride to
the surface…

… and sit looking out

at a sea studded with stars.

I am Oscar's best friend.

I am Oscar's only friend.

Where I lead, Oscar follows.

That's why it's up to me…

... to make a new friend,

so maybe Oscar can too.

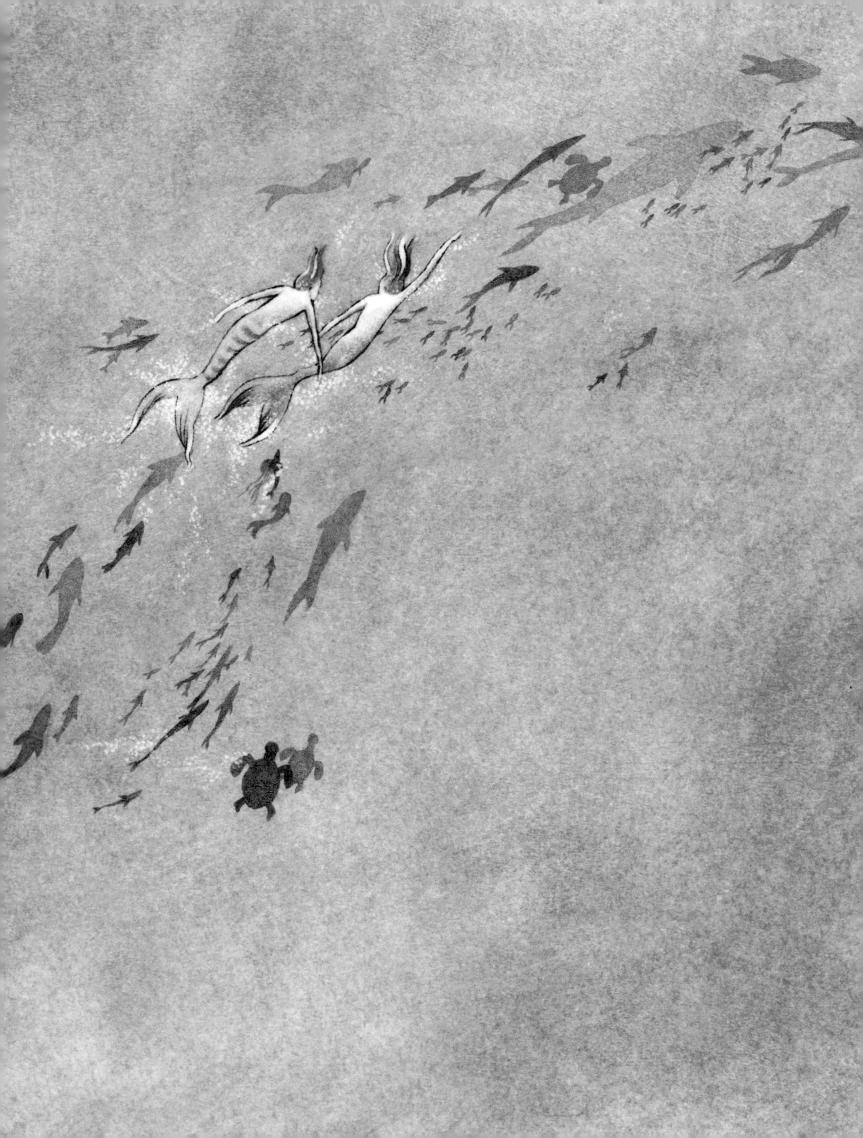